VIRION II

RISE OF THE SELF

DR. RAJESH VISWANATHAN IYER

Made with ♥ on the Notion Press Platform
www.notionpress.com

To the multifaceted Minds who pursue Biology, Psychology, Humanities and Digital Technologies. Contents of this book will serve to expand their appetite for fundamental knowledge on Human and Viral lives.

******

For the Generalists who dare to be Self-ishh...and always seek to broaden their Awareness.

******

Contents

Acknowledgements *vii*

Reader's Comments *ix*

Preface *xiii*

Prologue *xv*

1. Musings 1

2. Elemental Mind! 6

3. Elemental Brain! 20

4. Elemental Self! 30

5. Elemental Psyche! 40

6. Elemental Gnosis (awareness)! 44

7. Elemental Living! 50

Glossary 57

Acknowledgements

My sincere gratitude to all those who have helped me in the creation and publication of this book.

I am especially grateful to my Chief Editor, Meera for her insightful suggestions and unwavering support. I also thank my Beta Readers, S Viswanathan, Sonali Sarkar, and Rishika Iyer for their invaluable time and feedback through this process.

Special mention and thanks to Sanjuktha Pal for her consistent encouragement.
Thanks to all the readers for the enriching reviews, likes and comments towards the first book, Virion- An 'I' Story.

Reader's Comments

Reviews and Feedback for Virion - An I Story

- ***"Lucid and witty medical fiction by medical professional"***
- ***"Wonderful Read, A different perspective about virion"***
- ***"When a doctor says things as is, listen!"***
- ***"Captivating "***
- ***"What a navigation into our minds that can be a dark pit yet so sophisticated!"***

March 8, 2022, Rating 5/5

Lucid, witty medical fiction by a medical professional. The story flows effortlessly through the boundaries of physiology, psychology, geo-politics and age groups. Gripping story... I have read the book in one day!

Sanjuktha P (Senior Executive)

March 8, 2022, Rating 5/5

It's an awesome read, the flow in which the author has written is adorable.

A narrative is new and fresh and language in which it has been written is understandable to all age groups.

This book gives an alternative view about virions and its character and emotion.

My five star to the Book

The cover page is catchy and the title apt..

Awaiting to read more from Dr. RVI work..

Dr. Sonali S (Dentist)

March 16, 2022, Rating 5/5

A riveting view from the other side. RVI has kept the reader's attention throughout & very lucidly meshed science, medicine, politics & economic forces & how they dealt or responded to the pandemic scenario.

Zac M

March 13, 2022, Rating 3/5

Congrats Dr RVI. Unique piece of writing from the Virion's point of view. Great style trying to share science and philosophy together with a creative and imaginative approach. Kudos to your daughter and you for collaborating in this venture.

Dr. Shylashree E (Physician)

April 11, 2022, Rating 5/5

A doctor's take on a virus need not be a research paper. Doctor Rajesh Iyer has said more in 64 pages than any research on viruses could ever have. This review is intentionally spoiler free; the ending will make you recalibrate your perspective of life.

Jayachandran S (Entrepreneur)

September 20, 2022, Rating 5/5

Dr Rajesh has written such a wonderful book-- science writing meant for little girls and boys of class 5 onwards. Inspirational--for its writing style--imaginative in its

presentation--it is a wonder that for a psychiatrist--to write like this with so much care about their audience--this book has the potential to be a bestseller, to be nominated for excellent writing and can be beautifully moulded into an OTT movie or series.
Hope Amazon brings out a printed version to capture young readers and older readers alike!
Deepa J (Media Professional)

December 5, 2022, Rating 5/5

What a brilliant way to take us through our dark pit of minds and show us how sophisticated yet how unnecessary some things can be inside our minds.
Awaiting part 2! Way to go Sir, Dr.RVI ??

Amazing book, especially if our minds are undergoing rumination, consistent foggy thoughts. Fun reading this, felt so connected and witty at the same time.
Tara (Software professional)

Preface

Beyond Learning and Growing in Life comes the challenges of reacting to adverse effects of the ecosystems in our existential life. All along we are adapting to *controversions rather than to our own versions of Self.* From managing surprises of events to dealing with threats to our own self-composure, we are reacting. And there are so many aspects of existential and environmental Life, that we cannot be fully equipped or prepared to anticipate or expect full familiarity and predictability; at least not in one Lifetime.

The Pursuit of Certainty and Surety in Life seems so elusive and transitory after each milestone of success and achievement. We compensate for this *elusiveness* of the goodies in Life by symbolizing accomplishments. Symbolizing by collecting certificates, trophies, and memorabilia etcetera to authenticate the pursuit! Some of these pursuits, we strive to label as Success.

We sometimes dislike the **Nomadic nature of our Mind.** *Nomadic* because Mind loves and lives by Roaming after desires. We create identifications and possessions to keep the Mind and Body hooked or grounded with existence. We yearn to belong and attach instead of being with the ***flow of Life***.

Yet, our Mind's break free at times to embrace Nomadism, break Rules.

Elements of Uncertainty threaten the sense of surety and control established by the **Civilizational state of our Mind**. The Nomadic Self with Free Will becomes entangled and enmeshed with the mad voices and choices of the civilized state of Conditioned **Will**.

Prologue

Rifts between the *Nomadic Nature and Civilized states* of Mind leads to probabilities of distortions and disorders in the Psyche. **WELLNESS**, which is a byproduct of equilibrium and balance amongst the **ELEMENTS** of who we are is then at Stake (left to chance).

Beyond Learning and Growing starts the phase of Life called **PERFORMANCES** which puts every aspect of our Wellness to test. Our Roles, Our Choices, and Our Will to Exist are defined if we Survive....and get past the *Breaking points*.

Our **Minds** sometimes wait for opportunities or stranger things to happen before we start performing. And often we proceed in our Life stories with breaks, waits and waves of efforts.

Do we manage to keep our Elements together! If yes, How?

- by Dr. RVI

Virion was at ease until ANXIETY strikes......

CHAPTER ONE

MUSINGS

'I' recalled the predictions or wisdom bytes shared by Echo during the last starlink communication. I then tried to summarize Echo's message for me as a validation of my achievements. I finally listed the extract from the summary as follows...

- Regulated the impulsive qualities of the Mind.

- Patience is a virtue.

- Progenies future is a matter of many probabilities, only some likely facts can be anticipated.

- Association with Prion has potential for Great alliance in the future.

- Patient docs (my current home) future has no certainty or surety.

- Patient docs brain is my current womb, my psyche-spatial location from where I am supposed to evolve my Destiny.

This summary extract seemed to me like my Certificate of Existence (CoE).

Did I know my Cause of Existence!

Will my Destiny and my Fate be the same?

While I mused.......

A Voice within, deep from my RNA gene said, "Hello, aren't you here among Human civilization by accident?

Your basic roots are in the Wild, with Nature. With the Untainted purity that Nature presents, I would not like you to acquire the unnatural genes from this ecosystem and then become the toxic one among the current environmental versions or worldly variants."

I understood that this was the *Voice of Conscience*, from my Ancestral Gene. My ***Archetypal Identity***, perhaps.

Prion sent a message to alert me. "Archies (short for Archetypes) has no value or relevance in this current world. Ignore the Conscience. Archie genes are just comical. Be practical for this ecosystem. This Day and Age is beyond the time of Tin-Tins and Calvins. This is the Age...well if there is something named Seasons or Age anymore! There is no Climate anymore, just seems the world is going through the *Climax of a movie* called ***Time***. "

Prion continued while I wondered, "Let us say the current Time in Human world is about Day and Night and to be practical means existing on Insta-grams and TikTok's. And yeah, there is Twitter if you decide to get featherbrained on an issue."

Had Prion gone crazy with his Sabbatical or something, I wondered?

Who is Calvin, I asked?

Prion sent an emoticon with a round face, *laughing and crying* at the same time. Pretty complex, I felt. How could you feel both extremes together, can you?

Prion sent another emoticon which seemed like surprise or may be shocked or may be aghast; but before I could understand it got deleted. Why did he do that?

Was he mocking me or showing me the tricks of the **Tech-world**!

Prion said, "You need to learn a lot about the Digital ecosystem of humans. Their brains are increasingly influenced by the app-world and fit bit timers; less and less by inner logic or biological rhythms of the brain."

I understood nothing about what he was trying to educate me about. More so since Patient docs Brain was free and independent of the Digital ecosystem or its imprints, I was not experiencing Digital imprinting in his Brain space. His Brain was *Tech-Naïve*.

Regardless, Prion answered "Calvin and Hobbes were famous comic strip creations. Calvin, the main character demonstrated his intelligence through sophisticated vocabulary, philosophical mind, and creative talent. Supposedly Calvin did not have much of a **filter** between his brain and his mouth. He lacked 'Restraint', and not having the experience of the world to '*know the things that you should not do*'."

How is this changed from that Day and Age to this Day and Night scenario, I asked?

Prion sent an emoji with its tongue popping out and stated "Absolutely essential now to have filters in the apps and gadgets. Popup blocker and spam filters!"

He sent another emoji of a face upside down and tearing, not laughing, and said "These days having *filters in the Brain* is seen as being timid or a coward by nature (trait). Having filters between the Brain and the mouth is known as not having an opinion......and not having an opinion is like Death or Suicide on Social media."

To me Prions words sounded like a Conservative mind which is whining about Libertarian changes. I just listened and let Prion continue.

"**Self-Restraint** is not a virtue now. **Self-image** is dependent on the buzz users create on apps, posts that go viral at midnight and being a 'Troll' is like an emblem of **Self Identity**. For the Trolley humans, each opinion is like a Tesco or Walmart cart they have to fill with Pinions (O, which is the patience to wait a moment to think or form your own opinions is missing in the Trolls)."

"Every Pinion counts because all that matters is the number of likes, hearts, favorites, and forwards you can get Pinned on the page for the **Boogle** algorhythm to pick it up, amplify and trend it like a Wave which can be called '**Viral**'."

Bit irritated by the discourse, I retorted "How do these changes in Human lifestyle affect your Peace? Especially since you have such an Intellectualized Mind! Aren't you so adept and skillful in regulating your Mind and its feelings?"

Prion must have felt vulnerable after my retorting questions. Yet he composed his Self and responded with an emoji which was so confusing and *viciously mixed up* that I felt I could read or insert any feeling into it selectively and subjectively. Emoji's did not convey specificity. It was like a diarrhea of emotions from which I could pick up the emotional elements of my choice and of my prejudiced liking.

I wished for a feature called 'Disappearing emojis'. And wondered how Humans interpret the world of *emoticons* on their social media. They really must be for *Con's*. (Cheaters and Extortionists).

Prion read into my feelings of annoyance, sent a flower image and a message 'Disappearing feature coming soon.'

Prion was not one to run away from a debate or his Self. He explained "I am affected by the lack or deficit of **Climate** in the current Human Brains. It seems like their moods changed with Seasons of the Year earlier. Now, their **Moods** can changes multiple times in a day. The Social changes impacted their Nerves and Psyche earlier. Now, the *Digisocial* disorder impacts their Biological clocks and

Lifestyle rhythms. It feels like some process of *Reverse Engineering* is occuring on their Brain space."

I understood his dilemma about the future of the Human system as 'Does the Brain drive the Body or will the Body drive the Brain!

What is the solution, I asked?

Prions simple response "*Climate change* is not just an environmental phenomenon. It is an intraphysical (within body), biological and perhaps intrapersonal (within persona) issue as well."

What about Psychology or Psyche related changes, I queried?

Prion replied "I do not know that. Beyond my *Horizon of Senses*."

Prion had no intention of Gaslighting or Glib talks. And I liked him for his de facto nature.

I felt empathy for his larger concerns of Humanity but for now our habitat was Patient docs body, quarantined away from being **consumed by the Digi-social** order or disorder.

Prion has gone away from intra-neural (situated or occurring within the Nerve) communication now. I was left wondering how many Senses do we have! *Do Senses or Sensors within have Horizons*?

Without dwelling much on these, I was eager to start on my further journeys outside the Hippocampal area of the Brain. I have camped enough here. I needed guidance and some protection from Microglia, the policing cells in the brain. Are there smuggler type cells in the Brain?

May be a Spy could escort me or I need to get some training on **Neuropolitical mappings**. Seemed fabulous to acquire Neuropolitical understandings and then be like Prion!

CHAPTER TWO

ELEMENTAL MIND!

'I' waited. Sometimes expectantly, at times impatiently, many times boringly, often times directionless. **Wait** can be felt in so many ways and can be interpreted in so many ways by other's Mind. I was in a state of **Lock-In**, while my progenies were out in the human world evolving and doing their own things.

My **Progenies** were called Viruses. They carried bits of my genes and proteins in different combinations and proportions. Thus, different Versions, Variants and Subvariants were being made. They had differing Character *Traits*. Some of my Progenies were acquiring gene elements from Human Hosts. These acquired genes (Ag) were getting added to their Base Traits. In some Variants acquired gene elements (Age) modified their Natural gene elements (Nge) or Traits to form *Temperaments*.

I wondered what will be the future of my Genetic Legacy. Would my Progenies retain the genetic inheritance!

Some of these Gene Mixing and Gene Editing that was happening with my Sub-omicron Versions were producing Human body compatible variants. Some of them were acquiring corrupted genes from Human cells and forming *Extroverted* Temperaments.

As the Virion, I am different; complete and mature creation, Self Sufficient and could exist outside a host cell. I am independent of the Society of Human Cells. I can survive in an Active or Inactive State.

My current state of waiting made me feel as if I was out of existence; may be even cut away from my Instincts, Traits and Temperaments of the Mind. A thought of being '*Unreal*' was setting in.!

Prion sent a pop-up image, an image that seemed like Roboticon. Then followed his message "Have developed a chatbot. Yet to find a placement location for it, somewhere below the brain or base of the tongue! What do you suggest?"

I asked what was the need for such a thing called Bot. What will be the use case scenario?

Prion felt challenged by my ignorance and retorted "The future of Humankind is AI (Artificial Intelligence). With this Bot, Humans will be able to wag their tongue without bothering their own Mind. Internal processing can be outsourced to External processors of Machines. Machines will Learn while Human Minds can disconnect or dissociate from the hard realisms of Life."

"Instead of learning to bear weight of challenges, they can pay attention to beer bellies, beer biceps and frosting cognitive abilities." Prion dismissed me saying, "You are not with future reality yet". I did not care to react and followed my own muse of being Unreal.

Why Unreal? Because I was neither in the comfort zone of my Natural wild ecosystem, as created by Nature and I was not involved or integrated within the Man-made ecosystem, where I would multiply, mutate, and adapt. For me, my **Mental Life** had stagnated, quarantined inside the

Mindspace of a Patient doc.

Was I 'Ghosting' or 'Hibernating'. Is this how Quarantine feels like?

I realized that ***Mind always seeks the comfort of Belonging***.

Unattached or Isolated is not the permanent mode of Mind. The Quest of **Belongingness** can be outward (things, persons and Matters outside me). The Minds Quest of Belonging can be inward (Senses and Intel within me).

The patient doc was in an elementary state of Mind which means a **Base State**, Pure state, or Innocence. And he was in a state of Quarantine from the Society. An 'Unrealistic' state for him too!

I shifted my attention to Hospital ward. Resident doc seemed hopeful today. *But why do you feel hope for a Parasitic social status of Patient Doc?*
He had none of the **Spikes** needed to be part of or attach to Human Social Systems. Spikes like Money, Skills, Attraction, Power, Attachments, Legacy, Identity or even a Voice to Demand. He had nothing to offer and nothing to Expect.

Patient doc needed a **Personality**. He must come out of his Self-Effaced and Self-Absorbed state. His **Will** has to grow the Spikes which attach and *bond* us to Society and its systems.

Does Patient Doc (PD) have the will and intent for a Personality? If not, what can the Psychiatrist do!

Resident doc was waiting for the Psychiatrist to conduct the evaluation. The placement agency had demanded a Mental Health Evaluation report, which cited 'Clearance Protocol' before considering his discharge from Goodwill Hospital. Thus, he had an extended stay at Goodwill Services, for now.

I still wondered what **Clearance Protocol** means...*clearing the sickness, clearing the bills, clearing the insurance claims*! *Or clearing the will to do good*.

I heard the Resident doc reading news reports on how certain **viruses** (my progeny) were changing their *Spikes* characteristic through the process of *Mutations* in the proteins. The changing spikes helped the viruses to escape old antibodies and gave them the ability to attach to new types of cells and tissues in the body. These are called '**Escape mutations**.'

Resident doc turned around to the Nutritionist and asked, "Is this not similar to what we did as children to escape our parents expectations and punishments?"
The Nutritionist responded with a soft look onto his eyes, "Is this not what adults do when they want to escape the trials and heartbreaks of Love and Relationships?"
Resident doc turned away defensively and mumbled "**Pain**. We escape repetition of pain. And *Mutations in our Psyche or Mind* help us Rebel against Repetition of similar Hurt or Pain."

Nutritionist queried "Should we call Escape mutations as **REBEL** Genes then?"

Resident doc looked amused initially, then answered with a bright flinch on his face "*Jumping Genes*".

What the bluff, I thought. **Genes** are supposed to be the stable codes based on DNA.

Prions Neural image popped up showing "Just like software coding in the Digital realm."

The DNA of the cells are the biological core, something like the Skeleton in the physical body. Imagine the bony parts of the physical skeleton jumping around in the body. Wow. Break Dance of a new order, huh.

Well, the things that student docs might say to the other gender, while they try to flirt scientifically, instead of expressing the honest emotions of their fluttering heart. No wonder Doctors get wrapped up finding the Science of *Love and its Hormones*.

Prion interrupted "You are so off dated on Romance matters. Who does this kind of Mindful Love and Dating in this age? Mindless and less of Heart into Romance is the **New Age Mantra.** Humans make up for the deficits of Love by exaggerated gifts, vacations, and tattoos on their skins. Love is not even skin deep. In some parts of the world, Love is conveyed as a measure of how deep the tattoo is or how many piercings on the body parts."

I asked, what Humans mean by the phrase '*Love is in the Air*'?

Prion giggled then stated diagnostically "The phrase is a victim of Missing word syndrome. The real phrase is 'Love is only in the Air'."

Intellectually oversized and objectivity personified Prion who does not allow Emotions to cloud his Data analytics! How can Prion know about matters of Romance and Hearts! What can excess idealization do to *Mind and its Potential Emotions*. I mused.

Prion had hacked into my musings but simply reacted "**Over idealization** constrains Mind's Potentials. Elementary emotions and motivations can become suppressed."

Patient doc muttered "**Betrayal**". Abruptly, my attention shifted to the Goodwill ward.

To everyone's surprise, this was the first word spoken by Patient doc since his arrival in the hospital. Resident doc excitedly fired few questions but did not get any direct response from, just a **Reaction of the Mind** caused the formation of a small teardrop on patient docs (PD) inner angles of the eyes.

The Nutritionist said "Patience" as she gently placed her hand on Resident docs shoulder. "There must be hidden Trauma", she added.

I had a chance to correlate between the words, 'WAIT' and 'PATIENCE'. The difference in meaning was not clear to me perhaps.

I wondered whether Patient docs state was an **Escape from Trauma**. Could the cause be from the Mind or in the Brain.! Was the Trauma from his Past or Recent? Well, if the Neurologist did not find any evidence of Brain changes, maybe it is in his Mind, I thought. Trauma leaves *Encryptions in the Mind* called **Anticipatory Threats**, which becomes the basis for future Abandonment fears and Issues.

Does the *Mind mutate* to escape or to avoid the impact of unpleasant experiences of the Real World?

My progenies were mutating to avoid being destroyed as their fate. To survive and adapt now, for *coexistence* with Human Reality, they must constantly **Change**.

I wondered and imagined what would happen if Human species could mutate their mind and bodies to match the Wild animals. My progenies will not have to fight this battle of *Evolving to Survive*. Maybe I must say *Survival Development* because they were now losing their original envelopes and spikes to acquire and replace new ones; to become *compatible* and harmless to human hosts.

Either ways, for the pandemic to end one of the progenies has to transform: Human progenies or Virions progenies. *I did not know if there is a middle path, a path of mutuality (mutual evolution) to ease the end of the pandemic*.

We waited patiently for the Psychiatrist to arrive. A Nurse just remarked "Poor guy, they will prove him mentally unstable for the sake of justifying discharge from hospital. When the medical team does not have answer to medically undiagnosed or untreatable condition, they push the case towards Mental Health Basket. More like a Shunting out operation."

Well, in the **Jungles** among the animals, their episodes of illness, injuries and healing were more straightforward affairs. Games were played in the Animal Kingdom between different species, territorial battles were fought to preserve monopoly but the sick deserved grace and help from nature. Those animals at the bottom of the food chain were *natural parasites*. Those who were weakened by age or lacked courage due to their handicapped constitution turned **opportunists.** Over time the opportunists turned situational parasites, then adapted to being circumstantial parasites and finally progressed to become *parasites of nature*.

Parasites of Nature began evolving choices and behaviors which harmed and destroyed the nature that sustained and nurtured them earlier. In a way it seemed like they *turned against their Natural Self*.!

As I recalled the dynamics of the *Wild ecosystem*, I also tried correlating my memories of my old habitat with this *Civilized (human) ecosystem.* I could not correlate well to understand the meaning of 'Common Ground' between these two ecosystems. Perhaps there was none. May be Civilized is just another Jungle and Civilization just another human word.

Prion Insta'd privately, "**Scapegoating** may be the good word!"

I felt a desire to play Wordle with Prion everyday instead of playing Scrabble in my head while analyzing the World.

Prion gauged my thought and replied, “Not now. We are inside the *Scrambled Brain* of Doc. Cannot take too much *Data* Neurotransmission. Tsunami of *Stress* hormones may disorganize his Biological system.”

I asked Prion if I can contribute or collaborate with his work in any way. I wanted to help, participate, and aid in Docs recovery.

Prion said “Carefully, without replicating or reproducing, move to various parts of the Brain. Explore through different Spaces and Regions of the Brain. You will learn about the Structure and Connections in the Brain. Cautiously explore but hold back any temptations to experiment or interfere in anything. Be alert at border crossings between different regions of the Brain, specifically at Blood Brain Barriers. I will be monitoring and keep the Macrophages distracted from you.”

I wondered with mixed excitement if this was some Space exploration journey, or will this be like ‘I’ the alien immigrant trying to travel through the *United States of Brain* (USB). If I get caught, will I be deported or jailed in some Anonymous Bay or may be killed in the encounter. More so, I did not have an army or progenies with me to even mount combat.!

I decided to calm down the Apprehensions in my Mind. ***It was better to take Prions offer of Adventure than to stagnate, wait and die doing nothing.***

Apprehensions and my Imaginations became worse instead of calming down. I imagined situations of War between different regions of the Brain. What if the regions had their own armies and they had their own stockpiles of antibodies to start attack and counterattacks? What if they had their own sense of pride and nationalism? What if they had their old history of resentments and rivalries while each region of Brain was trying to develop and grow to their potential? What if they still have hidden ambitions of Supremacy? May be even *Supremacy Complex*!

Patient doc had been abusing alcohol in the past and perhaps has history of past trauma. What if he has atrophy or shrinkage of some region of brain? If those dysfunctional regions of the Brain have been least productive, will they have *Inferiority Complex*? Would they be hating the Economy of the more functional or productive regions of Brain? What if the **Cold wars** of the past turn **Hot wars**!!

Today might be the day, when their envy or resentments will come out in the open and trigger a war. I could imagine myself scrambling for refuge from one region to the other. Maybe I should enquire with Prion about any **Utopian Union** memberships or Treaties with peace keeping forces like GATO.

Prion questioned, "What is GATO?".

I replied, Global Acquisition Treaties Organization.

Prion quipped, "Really, is there something like that in Brain Space, Human Space or Wild Space? Wow...Never heard of that and don't think Patient doc ever heard something like that either. There is no such data in his Audio or Video archives in the Brain."

I felt upset. Was Prion mocking me! Did he not believe me? Or maybe he did not genuinely know. I was confused. A bit restless too.

Trying to **Rationalize** my fears, apprehensions, and sentiments, I started thinking 'So What' questions.

So what if there are conflicts and wars in the Brain. So, what if they had unwanted antibody stockpiles for deterrence and self-protection from invasion by unwelcome organisms. So, what if they had false pride and fabled nationalism. So, what if their old competing resentments and sibling rivalries of each region or state were activated now to elevate their potential by putting the other region down. So, what if hidden ambitions of Supremacy of Frontal lobe of Brain over Hypothalamus, or Right Brain over Left Brain surface as war to change the *Order of Importance*. Could the Hippocampus where I was residing in now, wage a war over of Supremacy over other Regions of Brain Space based on its Memory Capital and Rewriting the History, Right the Wrongs of Patient docs past and take Dictatorship of the future to avenge or revenge of the past betrayals. So, what....!

These questions were succeeded by 'What if' thinking and feelings.

So, what if the degeneration of Intelligence due to past trauma turns any region into *post traumatic poverty* of original thoughts or feelings and lead them to be overwhelmed by flashbacks or compulsive behaviors. So, what if the atrophy or shrinkage leads them to moronic collapses. So, what if the Inferiority complexes and envy leads to *fantasies of exploitation* of other regions and cold war conflicts. So, what if those Cold War's evolve into Blinding Hot Wars and *plunge* many regions of the Brain into depression, regression and suffering to patient docs body, mind, and spirit.

Stroke in the Brain can disrupt or block the Supply chain flow of Life Force Economy in the Brain and cause paralysis of the Body parts or whole body.

Patient doc as a Universe, mute and silent will suffer as if he has no Universal Will, Unknown as if he has no

Identity, Unconscious as if he has no stakes in Spaces of his Brain. His Ragged coat will always be a reminder that his spikes were removed or plucked out to prevent him from attaching or influencing the Societies of Human Civilization. He will be portrayed an Icon, only if can offer his services to the Goodwill Services Holding Limited. His Spike Potentials, along with his freedom to connect with Societies will be returned to him, only if he promises to surrender his Conscience to the Goodwill Group. He must forget to question "Why" and never hold mirror to the Goodwill Group representatives.

Goodwill Group is conditioned to look at matters around themselves, but never into themselves. This is Sacrosanct and embedded value into their perception and practice of Empathy.

I was shaking, felt tingling and numbing sensations in my spikes and coat. I needed Tranquility or a Tranquilizer. And I heard a slightly familiar **Voice of Echo**. "*World is One. Society is One. Brain Space is One. The Brain represents the Globe.*"

I freaked more and asked if my thoughts are not real. These possibilities are real, I emphasized.

Echo waited few moments and asked, "Where are you now? Are you aware of the surroundings?"

I retorted back at Echo asking whether he was Gorge of Sorrows? Was he War Run Buffets or may be Bull of Digital Gates? Could be Mark of Zucker (sugar) or a lawn of Musk growing grass (cannabis)?

I tried to observe but I felt clouded in my Mind. I felt things around me were unreal. Unsure and fragile.

Echo responded, "You are feeling a heavy state of Panic. Imaginations have taken over the functions of the Mind.

Apprehensions turned into anxieties, then escalated to fear. Fear and Insecurity is turning your Mind into a *Projection machine*, creating what is called by my Psychiatrists as '**Catastrophic Thinking**'. Catastrophic Thinking has spiraled up to extremes and now you are losing the differentiation between Normal, Paranormal and Real. Paranoid processes are setting in."

After some more silent moments, Echo continued "You are not wrong in your thinking or anticipation...but your imagination can take your mind too far, exceeding the limits of current possibilities. The fallout can be losing your boundaries of experience between the Intellect, Mind and Body. This creates **Psychosomatic illnesses**."

What do I do, I asked in an agitated tone?

Echo answered calmly, "At times like this, better to *Retreat and Re-evaluate* slowly. Adventures and impulses to relieve boredom do not bring desired solutions, always. Desperation makes things worse. First allow your Reasoning Mind to settle to its baseline or ground state. Flights of imagination will recede. Then look at your options like finding a Guide to explore the Spaces and Regions in the Brain. Prion is one friend, but does he have to be your only friend or Guide?"

There aren't any, I reacted with annoyance.

"**Have you really Searched**", asked Echo in a giggly tone.

I realized being too preoccupied rigidly around a few matters, which itself was too much new learning. It was foolish of me to embark on something else, entirely new out of mere excitement and no patience for preparation or groundwork.

I was now beginning to regain my Composure gradually.

While Echo was in contact, I asked him about his Perspective on my Imagined Wars in the Brain.

Echo as usual took a few moments before responding. Then spoke in a measured, serious yet compassionate tone "*Brain as a representation of the Cosmic sense* is yet to be truly understood by Science; science as perceived by Human Civilization now is still infantile. Before Scientific temperament grows further, Human Minds will need to shed their pride of accomplishments and be humble. Only then *new vistas* will open up."

What if they fall, I asked?

Echo resumed "Their fall is not important. Sometimes despite the fall the Pride and Ego does not shatter. At times the fall makes them more vain and blind to the *Cosmic senses*. A fall can turn them around like a **Boon** or make it worse like a **Bane**. Only their own Mind can determine the course."

I tried to interpret by stating 'So, the Fall is just an event which may teach the Mind to reconsider better Choices or give up Mistaken Choices.'

Echo in a corrective tone said "**A Fall or any other event of experience cannot teach by itself**. The Event becomes a Teacher only when the *Mind shifts* to a Learner mode. For this shift to happen, Vanity, False pride and Ignorance has to shatter. The nature of Event, the Context and the impact like a Rise or Fall become secondary. *Mind with its Intent and Will become the primary predictors of future Life course*."

I stayed silent, trying to absorb the unstated meanings beneath Echo's words.

"Addressing the specific question regarding *Wars in the Brain* which was in this case your Imagination running Riots of Thinking and Feelings. Was it exciting?"

I felt a bit of shame for being crazy during the episode. Echo sensitively commented, "***Mind is a Powerful instrument if you know how to harness it***, if not it is like a Horse that squirms but leads you nowhere special or specific. You did well with your Imagination. It was creative despite being dysfunctional to context. Do not beat yourself for it."

"Brain has evolved into different Lobes and Regions. Just like the Continents and Nations of Land space on the Earth. The different Lobes and Regions are important only for keeping them aligned and compact. Cells who perform identical functions and work in proximity, bunch together. The separation of regions by boundaries is mainly protective and administrative. Diversity is Real but only as far as each Region has a symbiotic give and take transactions and exchanges. No one region can survive on its own. If a region hits or exploits the other, it also gets hit in one way or another, immediately or with a delay. Brain stays the healthiest as long as the overall sense of Being One prevails."

I interpreted "So the Divisions are just a necessary part of Reality, but the **Truth is a sum of the parts**."

"Mathematically yes...but we realize these only when the Awareness of Localized identity periodically touches and retains the cosmic connect with Consciousness."

I wondered what is **Consciousness** but remained silent to learn about it another time. I was feeling well composed, even better than before I fell sick. In my Silence, Echo had also turned **Silent in my Mind**.

CHAPTER THREE

ELEMENTAL BRAIN!

I was wondering about Brain being the REAL ESTATE of the Persona, a <u>*Somatic Persona*</u>. Not a Psychic Persona.

Prion messaged "Welcome back."

I asked back to what?

Prion; "To Sanitized state of Mind" ...." And that too without any alcohol-based wipes, sprays, and swipes. Demand supplies gap went up for presumed Sanitizers like alcohols, Benzos, and Cannabis during the Pandemic in outside world."

Neurochemical modifying **Spirits** have substituted Mind moderating Spiritual tools like Meditations!

I; You don't miss an opportunity to poke. Why did you not prevent me from getting panic stricken?

Prion; "I can't get into your Mind, as long as you have Freedom of Will. Your **Free Will** is like a key to your own Consciousness. Unless you provide access to the key and grant me Command prompt to use it, I cannot enter beyond the *firewalls in your Mind*."

I; Like my Individuality. Why would I share access to my Free Will?

Prion; "Exactly my point. As long as you have your

Individuality, your Free Will guards it. Good or Bad, positive, or negative, is your doing, your matter of experience. I have no stakes in it."

I; So, you just watched me while all these chaos played out!

Prion; "I was preventing the disturbing impact of your chaos from spreading out and impacting Patient docs brain. Your hyperactive and decontrolled state could have set up Focal Seizure and triggered Generalized Epilepsy. This happens when there is derailment of electrical activity in the Brain. So, I was working to keep your sickness Quarantined."

And he added with a smiley, "Since you don't have a specific Assigned gender identity, I did not have to bother about possible **Gender war in the Brain**."

I did not know what to say, except thanks while I was feeling like a fool now.

I asked, "Why do we get Anxiety?"

Prion simplified the answer "Anxiety is like *Fever of the Mind*. Just like our biological body reacts to something it does not like or wants to get rid of by metabolizing (breaking it down), hence producing Fever physically. When the *Mind does not like some thoughts, emotions, or feelings*, it wants to get rid of the discomfort, confusion, or unpleasantness by breaking down, blocking, or cutting off part of those experiences."

"Parts of the Brain register these Anxieties from the Mind and convert these into Nervous experiences of the Brain. The Brain Neurotransmitters channel these to modify the Hormones which manage Stress and body Metabolism etc.... (Physiology of the Body)."

I impulsively asked, "Is there something called Dating anxiety!"

Prion shot back a nasty reply "Why are you getting such ideas now? You are too young, and Dating is a terrible territory to explore."

I felt Prion was having Parental anxiety or Big bro type protective anxiety for me. I had dated in the Wild Jungles. *My progenies will be dating in the Human ecosystem.* So, I had my Parental concerns!

Prion understood my ignorance and stated "Let's move on, untagged from past. The Psychiatry Consultant has arrived and is approaching Patient docs bedside."

Curiosity and quest to know excited me. I gathered my attention. Prion updated me that he has checked the Auditory channels of Patient docs ears and there were no snags or latency issues.

Prion sent me an attachment file which mentioned "The Broca's and Wernicke's area of Brain seem okay. Wernicke's area is responsible for the comprehension of speech and important for language development. Broca's area is related to the production of speech." ......" Earwax impaction leading to any blockage was cleared by the Nurse this morning."

Psychiatrist wore a Coat, a half coat. Prion corrected me stating it is a Suit. When I asked about the difference, Prion asked me to observe the Psychiatrist's functions, not her body and its armors.

Psychdoc with a Half Coat is how I wanted to name her. Psychdoc had impressive manners, organized, and composed in her approach to work. She read the patient chart presented by resident doc. She asked some historical questions and had discussions in the doctors room. As she walked towards the patient docs bed, she seemed thoughtful but composed. Upon reaching the bedside, she called him Mister and continued "I am here to evaluate your Mental health. I need to ask you some questions to help with this evaluation."

Patient doc made no movement of his head, eyes, or lips. He stared straight ahead at the window as if he missed the comprehension of Psychdoc's statement. She prompted, "Do you hear me, Mister? If so, would you indicate your reaction by moving your eyes or nodding your head!"

Patient doc seemed missing to react. I wondered if Psychdoc should stop calling him 'Misster' and use another word like 'Ureter' or 'Exeter'. Abruptly, a swallowing movement was seen on his throat.

Prion Insta'd me, 'Signals in his Memory areas indicate Recognition response. Patient doc has known the Psychdoc in the past.' I asked if she recognized him and Prion stated, not yet!

Curiosity and Hope within me raised expectations. I wanted her to recognize him, reveal his name, identity etc. Without his Past Memories, he seemed to everyone as a physically grown-up baby, living in the moment. With nobody around having a shared history with him, none of the humans in Goodwill space had deep seated attachment bonds. Except the Resident doc, who was forming an *empathic bond*, which was being considered Unprofessional.

Prion Insta'd, 'Unethical you mean!'

I wondered if there is a difference between Unethical and Unprofessional! Logically would unethical not be unprofessional.

Prion replied "Not in these times. Ethics and Professionalism are words, the meanings of which have been concocted and open to Interpretations of Convenience."

I queried "Would our doc be a victim of such toxic concoctions?"

Prion's lagging response was "Could be. But there are many people across professional domains who try to stand tall but are buried by the Goodwill Commerce of the Human society."

Goodwill Commerce sounded like an Oxymoron to me. Like a marriage of Contradictions. Well, who cares, I felt.

Prion reacted "In the *Context Now* of Human World, Goodwill Commerce, Goodwill Nexus, Goodwill Hunting by opportunists and Goodwill Sacrifice by Globally Ambitious Leaders is the Norm. The Left Brain of Humans harbors something and the Right Brain does exactly the opposite. *Split Brain* produces the **psychology of Oxymorons.**"

Wow, I thought. Prion gets the Neuro-psych correlations so well!

How does the **Splitting** of Left-Right Brain play out in Human Livestock, I asked?

Prion smiled and stated, "Not so fast Vir dear. *Brain literally represents a Mini Universe*. Parts of Brain represents Intellect and its functions, some parts represent the Mind's functions, many represent the Biological aspects of Body's functions. And there is a core areanamed **Pineal Gland** which represented Cosmic Consciousness, which is now present as a Vestigial accessory in the current variants of Human Species."

Prion paused and said, "When patient docs system recovers to full stability, I will set up a *simulation drive* for you to traverse and understand Human Brain. You will of course need an Invisibility Sheath to remain safe during the journey."

We shifted our attention outwards to the Goodwill Hospital ward with the Psychdoc reviewing medical reports and writing her own consultation notes.

I was anxious but the patient doc seemed blank, devoid of feelings or not letting them surface on his face.

Resident doc eagerly read the report, cross referenced some of the '**psychobabble**' terms and feelings on his face kept changing like a laser display of rainbow colors. His facial display went from confusion to surprise to anger, then sadness and then paleness.

Prion stated, "Micro expressions. Have you ever known face reading?"

I wondered what they were. Why would expressions be called Micro or Nano? Shouldn't expressions be just expressions and if not worth expression; feelings, and thoughts should be inhibitions!

Prion's emojified text was as if he was baffled by my ignorance. Then he said, "I love your innocence though it frustrates me." I felt timid and shy at the same time.

Prion continued "**An Innocent Mind** of the Baby expresses *basic emotions* and feelings freely; without Filters and Distillers to control, regulate, suppress, moderate, or form a dam around the feelings or thoughts. Either the virgin mind expresses freely or inhibits the instinct wholly. *No pre-judice* is involved in free associations. Abnormally, this occurs when an adult has Dementia of the Frontal Lobe of the Brain."

"In all other stages of human Mind, it learns to control the expressions by different ways of Mind management. These are called **Defenses**. Defenses help the Mind in modifying Expressions of thoughts, emotions, and feelings. *Modified expressions* can be Curtailing, Narrowing, Breaking it down and Scattering, Constipating or

Camouflaging the genuine content."

"*Simple emotions* are basic and universal, seen in all and are instinctive. *Complex emotions* are a blend of primary or basic emotions, just like the byproduct of mixing primary colors in art or painting. Also called *Secondary emotions*, these are a reaction modified to relate with an external person, situation or environments influence or context."

"These reactive expressions or responses modified by prior knowledge of something are expressed in 'Parts and Parcels', not wholly. This gives rise to conditioned expressions which are 'Fit to Context'. A liar will be managing his expression to fit to his context."

"These feelings or emotions and thoughts create **Data patterns** in the nerve transmitters in the Brain regions. Since the face is richly served by nerves from the brain, the fleeting expressions can leak even when the human is trying to suppress the display. These mini expressions can be emotional leakages **(Data Spill)** against one's will."

Wow, I wondered and asked "What if the Mind and Brain are dissociated or mis-aligned?

Prion replied," Then Emotions are not felt and not expressed or played out on face. Face is a representative of the Brain. Not the Mind directly."

"Is this the cause of Patient docs state now?"

Prion paused and stated, "We don't know enough about that, to conclude."

Attention shifted again to Resident doc who was now seen arguing with the Goodwill Service groups service manager and then his clinical services director. He was asking for grounds to extend patient docs stay in hospital for further treatment. The hospital said they don't have a protocol for his extended stay, and he must be discharged to the Mental health Hospital or to Homeless Shelter.

Insurance Services had already stopped payments to Goodwill group. An uninsured human, not in his amazing prime anymore, irrelevant enough to pay their Premiums for Healthcare access, no social bindings which could be exploited systematically by payment recovery agencies, was an unwanted Life; a tick in the register, waiting to be erased. The fate of his body perhaps a Medical college anatomy room, for dissection into fragments for Learning. Young students who dissected roaches and frogs might find this Person in Ragged Coat, amusing. Perhaps a steppingstone to their medical careers!

Resident doc was looking at the Nutritionists face and while his own face had micro expressions of turmoil and sadness, Nutritionists face was composed, calm and graceful. Their eyes locked in for prolonged seconds and she uttered, "Follow your Conscience and Heart, this time".

He asked, "Are you with me?"

She answered unhesitatingly "Yes".

Seemed like an ambience of **Crossroads** was being created, where many Lives would intersect to change; *for good or worse*. None cared, at least for now.

Diagnostic Report

The report from Psychdoc was transcribed by Lead Nurse for their Action charts. Gist of the report stated:

'No currently active Medical contributors',

'Recent history of Alcohol abuse – unknown duration',

'History of psychoactive substances (Cannabis, Cocaine etc) use or abuse – unclear',

Previously diagnosed Mental illness – unknown,

Prior Social history – not available.

Current laboratory tests:

Covid status - +ve on admission, currently -ve.

Blood tests – Normal parameters except mild Vitamin D deficiency.

Brain Scan – Indicative of normal imaging and functions except mild and patchy loss of grey matter neurons, likely alcohol dependence induced.

Neurological signs and reflexes are normal. No deficits

Current Impression:

Global Aphasia. (A disorder supposedly caused by damage to parts of the brain that control language.)

Differentiate from *Dissociative Identity disorder* with total *fugue.*

Recommend further Investigation – functional MRI scans. Neurologists follow up.

Treatment:

- Speech and Language Therapy.
- Family involvement is crucial.
- Evaluate further for appropriate Psychological therapy.

Resident doc was collecting information on possibilities of transfer to Mental Health units and Rehabilitation places. Most places declined on their reasoning that they were not equipped to care for such patients. None would state the diplomatic fact that without Insurance cover, they were not interested. State run hospitals required a government backed enrollment scheme to consider a place for him. *Goodwill administrators* were running out of their tolerance and were ready to tactfully shunt him out with his only belonging, the ***Ragged Coat***.

'I' just wondered whether the Brains of Goodwill Administrators shall be renamed as Goodwill *Predators* or Goodwill *Hunters* or just to be kind to them, call them Goodwill *Seducers*.

Goodwill groups will then look like part of the Jungle that I lived in, rather than the Civil society that I am trying to figure out!

CHAPTER FOUR

ELEMENTAL SELF!

The Nutritionist suggested tangentially, “What can you do for him, without scavenging the Healthcare system for possibilities?”

Resident doc mumbled “Take him home with me.”

Nutritionist: “What are the consequences?”

Resident doc: “I am not applying my Intellect to evaluate him or the consequences.”

Nutritionist: “In a world where every little thing is decided on consequences, can you afford to choose by your Heart? Think of Medico-legal angles.”

Resident doc: “This is not a matter of my Heart only.”

Nutritionist: “What is your sense of connect with him then? Feelings, displaced emotions...or some ideological thought of beneficence! Perhaps some utopian value of Selflessness?

Resident doc paused long into a Silent mode, then said “I don’t know”.

Nutritionist lounged backward and sipped her Herbal concoction, thinking to herself if this was some **Magnanimity of his Soul** matter. Omnipotent fantasy or **Messiah complex** as they call it.

Nutritionist: Are you thinking about the Ethics issues, the adverse impact, or risks to your Professional career?

Resident doc: "Soul dwells on Principles. Ethics are based on Matters of Intellect's Values. Morals are from Matters of Reason's in the Mind."

Nutritionist: "So which one are you inclined to align with?"

Resident doc: "The world and society won't care what I align with. They will only see the Human factors that I betrayed."

Nutritionist: "Since it is impossible to blend Principles, Ethics and Morals in the current state of the world, you can possibly only choose your Alignments. Invariably, we are all Betrayers of what we did not choose.!"

Resident doc: "Our **Inner Self** is constructed of many strata or layers. Each of these can be understood as platforms with interconnecting portals. Yet the world sees only the e-version of our existence; the *farce book* and the *tweaker apps* of social mediums."

Nutritionist: "**Self is Inner and consists of Spheres** just like the Atmosphere around Earth which has five layers; Troposphere, Stratosphere, Mesosphere, Thermosphere, and Exosphere. If these strata disconnect, and leaves a vacuum in between, *dissociation* can set in and cause unwanted consequences to the Personality of the Earth."

Resident doc looked at her eyes and they both laughed at the ridiculous expansion of their conversation now.

Nutritionist said, "***Session over***. But you are keeping me in confidence and in sync with the decision you make on this case."

A nurse walking by got some hint of this dialogue and stopped to ask, "Would you not try to know his religion before deciding?" The Nutri-doc duo sprung up from their seats and left hurriedly.

Prion Insta'd "Nutri-doc duo are **Atheists**. They believe in God but not the theology on God."

Echo's voice amused me, "*Prophets and messengers elaborated on God to unite Humans, yet the byproducts of their impact called **Religion** divides Humans*. Another **Oxymoron** perhaps."

'I' worried and wondered about my progenies, alpha, beta, gamma, delta, epsilon, mu, and omicron. Mildly I regretted the irrational reproductive behavior of mine in the past. When I was new to the human ecosystem, did not know much about the realities and dynamics in the human realm, why did I reproduce so fast. Why did I have such high reproduction rate or **R factor**?

Prion sensed my discomfort and messaged in private, "You were innocent. And you were naturally very fertile. Historically, Humans had high reproductive rate. About 100 years ago, human families had 10 – 18 offspring on average. During a mythical phase of time called Dvapara, preceding an epic called Mahabharata, a queen called Gandhari had 100 children."

I wondered why I had more fertility rate than my other Virion cohorts. May be this was okay for the Wild woods and the Lifestyle there, but not appropriate and a misfit here in this ecosystem. I hoped my progenies would become aware and tone down their R factor.

My Life now was celibate within the body of patient doc. Quarantined for a good cause!

I asked Prion, if he had any advanced communication technology to facilitate my contact with my progenies.

"**Starline** might be possible, but you need approval from Echo to activate it. I can do the deployment of firmware between the Mind and the Brain", replied Prion. Then added, "Starline is a new technology in fifth dimension

(5D). This is in design phase, so be patient."

One of Nurses was reading the newspaper article about the ongoing Pandemic, close to patient docs bedside. The first **Gen virus**, Alpha, was not prominent anymore. Beta was not a concern. Gen Delta had caused major adversity during the peak of its wave. Gen gamma and others did not transmit like a pop star image and were mellow or subdued. Gen Omicron transmitted fast and widely, caused sickness but ebbed (subsided) quickly. Now there were concerns about **subvariants** of Omicron combining their genetic material.

I wondered if that would be called ***Incest***. Mating within the subspecies or subfamilies may cause combination of Strengths but could also pass their individual weaknesses to be reinforced on transmission! Is this called Hybridization?

Hybridization among Human Chromosomes and Genes create subfamilies of their Body Coat based on Race, Caste, Ethnicity!

What may happen if Alpha, Beta, Gamma, Delta, and Omicron keep mating, breeding, and rebreeding among themselves? Mixed breeds or Mixture of Breeds....and as I was Humming over my Whatsup thoughts...I heard Echo "Scientists have named your variants as **Recombinants**."

Prion telegram'd "Matter of Conjectures, rather than Science. Don't dwell on these. Though *Corrupted genes* from parent viruses can produce more corrupted progenies through partial or full reinforcement."

I asked, What is the solution to prevent this random hybridization and remove *corrupt progenies*?

Prion telegram'd, "Selective Hybridization. But it is not easy to enforce this regulation."

I reflected on whether to blame myself or consider these events as *THE FAULT IN MY STARS......*

I wished some sort of Power in me could curtail my Progenies fertility or reproductive instincts.

Prion felt discomfort with where my thoughts were going. He cautioned "These thoughts and correlations could take you into the loop of regret, shame, and guilt. Remorse is the outcome of such processes."

Prion continued "Star links and Star wars with a focus on Fault finding is best done under ***Divine guidance***. And I have no experience of those ***Spiritual matters***. I may not be able to stabilize you if you slide into Crises of Self-Worth or Self-Esteem from Inferiority Complexes."

I agreed with Prion and decided to refocus on **Goodwill Ward** and patient doc for now.

As discharge process was being finalized, resident doc was discussing and documenting the discharge diagnosis with his team. And I jumped closer to the auditory nerve terminal for better hearing and clarity of understanding on **Dissociations.**

Dissociative disorders include effects like **Amnesia** (loss of Memory of facts, information and experiences), **Fugue** (state of extreme confusion with a loss of a sense of subjective persona and wandering or travel away from the established habitat), **Depersonalization** (state of intense feeling of disconnect or detached awareness between an *Individual's sense of Self, Mind and Body*), **De-Identification** (state of splitting of Characteristics of *Self and Ego* mediated Personalization). A fragmentation (fracture like process) of Persona may be causing Multiple Personality disorders.

Lead discharge Nurse found these too complex to understand and asked, "What is the cause and what is the likely future of 'Ragged Coat' (referring to Patient doc)?

"Severe emotional **Trauma** which impacted deeply within the **Unconscious** realms of his Mind", responded the Resident doc. Nutritionist continued, "**Dissociation** is like the Breaking of the Self Identity, similar to the Fracture of the Bone in the Body." Neurologist added, "The Brain level *Neuro-circuits* may show damage over time."

Resident doc stared upward, towards the ceiling and said with a sigh, "Future recovery is undetermined. If we hope, it could be months, years or never in this lifetime. Healing is possible...but external care is not enough, unconscious inner Intent from his *Superego* will need to respond. **Intent and Will to exist matters!**"

I Whatsupped Prion, "Do you agree or validate this psych evaluation?"

Prion answered "Yes...but there is more".

How do you know, I asked?

Prion: "Before my entry into patient docs body / brain, my previous host was a known **Serial Killer**. He had Dissociative disorder with psychopathic features. Dissociative disorders, multiple personality disorders or Split personality disorders, whatever the human diagnostic manuals may call it is still not fully understood. *Personality dysfunctions and Identity disorders are a different Universe,* yet to be studied fully and elaborated." ......" **Trauma does have the potential to cause Reverse Programming of the Mind**. Conscious experience can change or mutate the subconscious and unconscious elements of the Mind and Self."

I grew more curious about the Universe and wanted to ask Prion about his story of escape from a **Serial killers Brain**! But I deferred that Curiosity for another opportune time.

Echo emerged abruptly "One of the most common and overpowering Split is the Polarization of the Mind between the **Will to Love** and the **Will to Hate**. This Internal polarization at the Unconscious realm of Mind becomes a *breeding place* for Disgust, Resentments and Contempt."

Echo confirmed that the consequence of these *inner breaks* within the Psyche is externalized as **Psychopathy and Sociopathy**.

I asked Echo, "If these processes correlated with Patient docs **Rigged state of Mind** and his Ragged Coat existence?"

Echo said "May be or maybe not. Be Alert and Observe."

Well, The **Enigma** continues, I thought to my ***Self***.

Resident doc got an angry call from his Supervisor and Hospital manager of Goodwill group. He was asked to change the Diagnosis to something more acceptable. In the transfer politics of healthcare network and healthcare agencies, including Insurance companies, diagnosis is modified to adapt to their policy manuals. Of course, manuals of convenience and profits. Certain diagnoses are easily billable! Billability and Profit margins determines which diagnosis is applied.

Resident doc asked in frustration, "What is an Acceptable diagnosis, in this case scenario?"

The command was "Diagnosis that will make another hospital, Rehabilitative center or Homeless Shelter just accept the patient for transfer. So that we can discharge him to get rid of him."

Resident doc hung the phone, as well as his head for few moments. Then turned to the Nutritionist with a tilted face and blurted in resenting tone, "*Hypocrite's Oath* is what we take in this career. It just is misspelt as Hippocratic Oath!"

Nutritionist tried to keep her composure despite feeling the upset and said, "Masking the Intent is a very common defense of the Mind. May be Freudian Slips of words and unconscious verbiage existed long ago before Freud."

Resident doc walked away for a Coffee shot while muttering "Masking of Intent is an Offense of the Mind. Whosoever named it a defense was perhaps a sickly dishonest man, inclined to condone his own compromise in Morals."

I felt sorry for Patient doc. So did the Nutritionist. I what's upped Prion for his feeling.

Prions reply was "I feel nothing moral or immoral. I work with facts called Data in the Brain. The **Digital system** or for that matter the **Neural system** is not the *Morality keeper* in the world. Nor am I the *Conscience keeper*."

I felt annoyed and wondered, "Where is empathy?"

Echo stepped in as if to prevent a dialog between me and Prion. "Empathy in the current version of Human Minds is 'A Lost Word'. In many compartmentalized Minds, it is *a fossil now in the Museum of their Intellects*. Empathy is considered a dangerous trait to have by many Human Variants. The rationed or filtered form of empathy experienced or displayed by some of the Human variants is called Sympathy."

Echo continued "Sympathy by itself is a tool for Trade and Transactions, now."

I asked Echo about my Progenies and Generations of Variants and their **Actions in the world**.

Echo answered, "*Delta* had very little sense of Empathy. It's Instincts were Raw and Wild. It Reproduced and Replicated fast, without a sense of Family Planning. But *Omicron* did receive Light from the Universe and modified it to not cause fatal damage. Omicron attempted to be graceful. Other versions like *Beta*, *Gamma*, *Mu* etc did not have the interest or inclination to be too competitive or to Dominate the Viral ecosystem. Your Progenies and offspring do not have Free Will, but they do have the Nature's gift to adapt to their hosts' nature. The hosts in this scenario are Humans, with Free Will."

I asked if that meant Humans could adapt to tolerate the Viral variants!!

Echo affirmatively stated, "Yes, they have the **'Equity share' in the Natural world, to adapt, accommodate and co-exist**. 'Living with the Virus' cannot be a catchphrase to defend their incompetence's of the Mind. Nor should this phrase be a slogan to Mask the Intent to profiteer and exploit the vulnerable and less fortunate among the species."

I reflected whether these would count as Offenses of the Mind, as Resident doc articulated.

"Defenses were applied to protect Self from external experiences which are injurious, adverse, or traumatic to one's own **pristine self**. Then there was a time and phase where Defenses were applied to protect others from our inner **Angst**. Now they are applied to cover up our own **O**ffenses, **L**ies and **D**ark wishes." These were the parting sentences from Echo.

Defenses are employed more for practicing and aiding the art of Deceptions. I interpreted this and Prion What's upped me with a smiley 'Bingo'.

As usual, I had a confusing Question and shot it to Prion. *Why do we call the Self-protective instincts and attitudes*, Defenses? Should they not be considered *fences* or *firewalls*!

So, what is ***Self*** in simplest words without the descriptions, offenses, defenses etcetera?

Prion seemed blank. I waited in silence for an answer. From this Silence of the Mind emerged the Voice of Conscience. "Self is the way the Cosmic Forces put me together (assembled my Soul, Intellect, Mind and Body). The Original Version of the Divine, without the variations and mutations made by experience of the World."

Prion dived in with his analogy to boost this perspective. "In the **Digital realm**, Self is like the digital device straight out of Apple or Microsoft factory with *factory settings* before the consumer or customer activates it for use and chooses to modify the settings."

Are there Cosmic settings for the Self?

CHAPTER FIVE

ELEMENTAL PSYCHE!

Prion had a jibe at me before digging into history. "Vir dear, aren't you becoming too *analytical*?"

"**Psychology** does not have to become *Archeology* of the Past or History. Mind can consume you by luring you into the *Fantasies* of the Past. People start dwelling in the past recesses of the mind. Some experience *regression* and a disconnect with present and future realities of Life. Bear this as a friendly reminder."

Prion proceeded further with his perspectives as a digger into **History**.

"As far back as I can regress into the History of Modern humankind, which is perhaps a few thousands of years. **Legacy data** from my ancestor's genetic pool extends only for this era. Any memory of humankind's previous experiences before 2000 AD were discarded by my forefathers from that time."

I asked why would they delete history? Isn't history precious? Does it not inform our present and future choices? Does it not make us who we are today?

Prion sent a frowning emoji and asked me to hold my horses in my mind.

"Historical data that is genuine comes with a validity cycle. During this phase Data is genuinely recalled, recorded, and transmitted. This is termed **Data Fidelity**, which in the Brain (Hippocampus) of Humans, or in the genes of the Prions is registered as **Core Memory** or *evolutionary memory*. Humans call this **Knowledge**, which is the Memory of what has been known and experienced before now. Such knowledge is lost and found, forgotten and rediscovered or sometimes destroyed and reinvented. This process leads to an external state of **Delusions in the Mind**. In Sanskrit Language, it was called *Vikruthi*.

"During the above processes, with reformations and variations of knowledge pool, **gaps** are created in the data pool. This is filled by future generations, by imaginations, distortions or whims and fancies of what could have been. Many times, over, in the past, **Histories** have been recreated or reimagined to use them as a tool or product to achieve mean **objectives** like winning *wars* of perception, *deception* to bring down a prosperous community or civilization or an Icon. History also erodes or rusts."

"*My ancestors decided to dump historical data, whenever they realized that the legacy data is contaminated, mutated, and misinforms future progress*. That's when History has become an unhealthy baggage to bear or rely upon!"

Echo sounded grim "***Relevance of History*** is associated with its functionality in current design of Life and constructive evolution of Mind. *Corrupted* knowledge is like a bug that destabilizes the *Self* systems first, then turns cancerous and enacts **Illusions** in the Mind and Brain."

Does it mean we must *discard toxic history* voluntarily, I asked?

Echo and Prion said 'Yes' and added "This is how ***Survival of the Purest*** has occurred from time to time. **Memory detox and Data detox becomes the Soul option when the baggage bogs your Mind down.**"

I wondered how my Progenies will detoxify from the excess of experiences and the reverse impact they are acquiring from the human ecosystems. *What if they internalize some corrupted human genes and contaminate their pure virionic genes*? Will they become half Virion and half Human in their traits and temperaments!

Prion giggled, "Now don't imagine your progenies to be like Mermaids, or become Viro-humanoids (Half virus and half Humans)."

I wondered, why Humans are working on Humanoids (half humans and half robots)?

Echo intervened this time "Your creative imagination is very fertile. A strength of yours this Lifetime but going overboard perhaps!"

I promised to watch out for wild interpretations of my Mind.

Prion continued "**Languages** have gone through similar mutations and variation over the period of invasions by empires. Some meanings of Latin words or Greek words or Sanskrit words are now not just derivatives of the original.

Gnostic senses which formed the basis of language formation were degraded and diluted by Agnosia. Original meanings became debatable and gradually endemic versions of the original parent languages established themselves. Opposite meanings emerged like oxymorons. This is called **Debasing**."

What is Gnostic sense, I asked?

"Gnosis is the Greek word for INSIGHT. Gnostics believed that humankind contains a Divine spark within themselves. This spark from Consciousness descended into other realms of semi matter and then the physical matter, which is like extension into another external realm."

"Gnostic senses have a top-down or Inside Out **Cognition order** of Ceptions and Perceptions of Universal processes and creation. Paradoxically, **Science is relatively Agnostic to this Universal order**."

Gnostic senses involve Insight through connect with fields of Superconscious Energy fields. These energies emanate directly from Universal Consciousness. Soul is a tool in this context and receives the power of Ception.

Intuition is the next sense of perception. Soul is an originator in this context.

Intellect and Thought forms and Streams are the next Senses.

Mind with its Emotions and Feelings add to the extending realm that the Spark descends into.

Biological forms and bodies are considered as senses that embodies these inner Senses and Sense Abilities."

I was fully consumed and confused by **Prions perspective**. But I did not want to show or expose my confusion or ignorance. So, I sent few emoji's like smilies, thumbs up and hugs. I knew I was pretending, but that is what *tech media* empowered me to do. Much more *easily and shamelessly* than if I had to pretend with Prion in direct physical interactions without tech.

Echo intervened here "Stark realization Virion!"

CHAPTER SIX

ELEMENTAL GNOSIS (AWARENESS)!

"**Gnosis** in the beginning of Humankinds time cycle was purely about **Souls** enacting their Role play in the *Cosmic scheme* produced by Consciousness. Consciousness directed the play of Virtual Realities and Augmented Realities. The Biological and Physical bodies were experienced as Augmentation.

I asked, "Augmentation of What's going on?

Echo corrected patiently, "Augmentation of **What's In** each one of us. Astral Reality."

Echo Continued......as I stopped Interrupting.

Insight was Divine, or *Consciousness based* for every Soul which expanded their existence and descent into Human realm and its bodies. *The World was One*.

Some who gained more prowess by assimilating *Universal Energies* were able to expand more efficiently into their AR (Augmented Reality) and VR (Virtual Reality) Avatars. They became dominant yet were compassionately nurturing the others who were taking more lag time in evolving their expanded *Avatars* or what is also called *Persona*.

Frustrations and some resentments about their own setbacks to the process of successful evolutions started creeping into some Souls. This *angst* further started retarding their pursuits, instead of helping them succeed.

Economy of Energies did not seem Equal anymore.

Some of the frustrated Souls wanted to practice DIY (Do It Yourself) and found the Consciousness to be a constraining parent rather than an aiding protector and guide.

They wanted **Free Will** for their Pursuits of Independent growth. Thus, the concept of **Individuality** was born on the premise of *Agnosia from Consciousness*. Or they could seek Voluntary Gnosia of Divine, as and when required by their Free Will and **Intent**.

This batch of Souls relied on their *Own Core*and experimented to evolve further. But gradually, their access to Gnosis from Consciousness became dimmer and lesser. In Sanskriti, this was called Dwaita (Twosome or Dual) mode of *Existence*.

Consciousness instructed the **Aligned Souls** with prowess and a successfully evolved Persona and Human existence to guide those others with Free Will; *if they falter* during existential efforts.

These well evolved and powerful Souls who were constantly enlightened by Consciousness began evolving **Systems of Guidance** and support for each *Realm of existence*. At this stage, more and more Souls as different groups were asking for Free Will as a mode to explore, expand and evolve their pursuits of success."

I couldn't hold back the Horses in my Mind though my Mind actually felt like a Donkey standing still out of Ignorance or Innocence. I enquired sheepishly if *the*

Guidance systems are the same for each Realm of Existence? Echo just stated **NO** and then proceeded with his Course of Narrative.

"The result or consequence of these allowances were increasing *Diversity*. The Diversities and the probabilities of Humankind based differences and divergences gave rise to different *endemicities and ethnicities*. The Human bodies shaped out differently based on the **Souls choices** which informed and impacted the mutations and variations of their Genes."

"Individuality gained and sustained as their Identity, started leading to further *Agnosia of Cosmic Energies*. But those Cohort of evolving Souls still looked up to the Souls who were connected with the **Cosmic Gnosis**, who were then called Wisdom Souls, Gods, then Gurus, then Masters, Teachers, Prophets etc. over the Time cycles called Ages."

"Some of the Souls were not content with their existence and in comparison, to others not equally successful. This created the scope and possibilities of comparative Self Worth, Self Esteem and Competitive Pursuits and imaginations of Success. *Seeking inspirations and Validations from outside became more of the norm.*"

"**Insight** diminished for these Souls and **Power of Ception** was lost. Thus came the need and want for other forms of communication like Thought Forms, Ideologies and Language of Words. These came to be known as **Perspectives.** Intuition of Souls did not effectively transmit to the existential realms like Intellect or Mind. This led to Persona's breaking free from their own Soul's influence and monitoring."

I wondered if this was a form of Dissociation between the Soul's Ception and Intellect's Perception! I kept mum and held back the Question to my Self, letting Echo continue...

"Growing resentments and dissatisfactions, resulted in envy, disgust, greed to encroach on other individuals achievements, to dominate others by craft or by force became part of the Intellects Perspectives. Good versus Bad replaced the Cosmic sense of existential Gnosis. *Agnosia of the Value* systems of the Intellectual existence led to *pretend games* to conceal shame, lowering Self-worth and negative esteem from acting against their *own Conscience.*"

"**Minds resented** the constraint of their own Intellects prohibitions or constrains against Freely pursuing Emotional wishes, desires, and indulgences in excess. Expanding powers and prowess of the minds required *Agnosia of the Intellect* and breaking away from Logic based existence."

"Souls and Intellects became supporters or bystanders while the *Mind based Existential living* took over the mantle for driving and imagining the pursuits of evolving the Personalities, Avatars and bodies."

"Intellectual existence and its diverse priorities had divided the World Image within Individuals. Yet the Contradictions within were managed by *Common Purpose and Existential goals.* This is how communities and families kept their flocks together. This became the basis of **Elemental Societies.**

Multiple divisive Images to match multiple situations caused more **Compart-Mentalizations** in Mind. *One Mind did not operate like One Nation anymore*!

"Humans, until this time were Religion Agnostic. Divided Perspectives and Beliefs created a deficit in receiving Universal Value systems uniformly. In the absence of direct Cosmic connect during later stages of Human Succession, Prophets and Messengers took birth in different Communities and Sections of populations. **Religions** were thus Born among Humankinds need for 'Holding together' perceptions and 'Organizing Thoughts' into a **Schema for the Mind.**"

"Religions were meant for communes or sects and hence **Secular** in motive. Religions were never meant to become Empires through Interconversions. RE-LEGION was and is a temporary channel of Gnosis: for receiving some knowledge, some assurance, and some comfort from Cosmos. This temporary reverence of any RE-Legion must have the end goal in sight, which is Connecting again with the **Legion of Cosmic Sense** (Cosmic Awareness)."

"Agnosia of their own Intellectual Senses by the Mind, led to the **Power of Perception** being the dominant sense. Perspectives and Logic were lost or messed up. The tool for Perception was efficient and clear **Reasoning** of the Mind's experiences. Reason was a filter for differentiation and choosing between functional behaviors and dysfunctional behaviors and choices of Personality."

"Mind based Existence became the basis of Self Awareness and Self-image. Conscience and Idealism became a Memory which was objectified in the form of symbols, idols and to be understood in new forms in physical realms. The **Cosmic Gnosis** is now sought in material realm as objects such as stones, territorial locations, icons etc. Humankind is busy recreating the "The Lost Gnosis of Inner Order and resources" in the externalized existence. The awareness of the Minds were now being limited to the conscious world while much of their own Mind and its Potentials have become Subconscious and Unconscious to their own *Individual Perceptions.*"

"Minds have filled their awareness with experiences up to the brim, become hypersensitive and hyperreactive, finding it difficult to maintain a check on functional pursuits."

I flipped inside me wondering if I had become an **HSP** (Highly Sensitive Person) or rather HSV (Highly Sensitive Virus). I maintained *Sush in my Mind* instead of flushing out my feelings of the Mind.

"Minds are finding it difficult to maintain fences around their choices, goals, and instincts of purpose. Their *mental self-image* is under constant threat of effacing and flummoxing under social pressures and expectations."

*The default self-protection tools called **Defenses**, are employed when the natural Fences of Self Resilience are not in place or not working functionally enough*.

I wondered if the **Mental Health** was an Issue of Emoting or Issue of Living.

CHAPTER SEVEN

ELEMENTAL LIVING!

"Individual Minds of many Cohorts of Humankind have turned *Agnostic to Reasoning* as a sense of their Free Will. Emotions and feelings are their drivers of existential routines, pursuits, and expectations."

"Brains of many cohorts of Human forms identify their existence as physical matter and bodily existence. Their Brains have become *Agnostic to their Minds*. **Brain and Brawn are their catch phrase of Self Image description.**"

"**Brain** as the driver of Insight now and Body and its senses as the pursuer of Free *Will* and its consequences is the reality of the current **Human Realm**. The means of transactions are monetary, goals are physical procurements and hoardings of physical pleasure."

"Emotions and feelings are considered as impediments to uninhibited pursuit of mindless and excess materialism. For the **Insights of the Brain**, everything is pure matter. *Mind is now conceived as a product of the Brain functions*. Consciousness is being researched and theorized by Scientists as a *byproduct* of Brain Regions and its Cortex."

Perceptions today are receding to be a Gnosis of Neuro-linguistic-sensing and programming.

"Agnosia of the Brain and Bodies senses has started as an existential cohort in Human forms. Ignorance of the nature of Human bodies and its fundamental requirements for upkeep and maintenance has resulted in *Brainless abuse* and dysfunctional choices towards physical existence and awareness of natural requirements. *Agnostic behavior towards Science* of biological and physical bodies is evident during the challenging pandemic."

Cogito ergo sum is being replaced by Digito ergo sum, as a source of perspective.

"*Digital Gnosia* is the current new emerging world. The unorganized and unsystematic order of the Internet manifests as unruly diversity of content and consumership. Sanctity of *Inner Gnosis* is a dead idea and so is Human forms quest for Gnosis and knowledge."

Digital Gnosia is the new Driver and Influencer of FREE WILL.

"Digital footprints and *Digital Image* are fast becoming the **paradox** of *Self-image*. Digital photoshopping and Social media tech appears *Agnostic to the Personality* of the user. **Perceptions** are created to erect, salvage, or destroy the image, reputations and relevance of Individual's opinions, ideas, or values. Emotional conflicts and vengeance effervescently flow through the digital realm of our existence. Scientific opinions are now gathered through digital surveys, ratings and web curriculums which offer digital certifications on various knowledge matters. Knowledge and physical *effort-based economy* is in ruins while the 'Make money while you sleep' kind of catchphrase is gaining ground as the frontrunner model of businesses of Life."

I wondered why Echo uncharacteristically chose to provide an Epilogue on Gnosis and Agnosies? It felt fascinating and overwhelming at the same time. Felt the need to hear it again to absorb and grasp well.

Prion messaged "I have got this on record in a special drive."

Virion: Did you not know all of this, based on your Gnosia?

Prion sent a wink emoji and replied "I am not so omnipotent that you might think of me! Besides, my Gnosis is limited by what Human Brains have known in the last 2000 years. I read and gain Gnosis from the **Neurological memories** and data in the Brain and Nerves cells."

Virion: Where does Echo gain the Gnosia?

Prion: "Perhaps, *Cosmic energies*, I guess. You must ask Echo if you strongly wish to know. I usually go into a Receiver mode of Intelligence whenever Echo appears and communicates his **Broadcast**."

Prion informed that he observed some specific activations of electrical signals in **Pineal** gland region of patient doc while Echo was delivering the Epilogue on Gnosis. He needed time and solitude to research into that strange and phenomenal data.

I shifted my attention to patient docs human realm and Goodwill hospitality's not so good intent towards healthcare or Human Care.

Looking at the *Pixelated* version of Human World's Image, I wondered in contrast mode how and if the projection of *Echo's Gnosis of an esoteric realm* would look like? If such a realm was part of the Human experience or did the current generation of Humankind evolve and fallout of such realms? Did Human forms become an *Outcast* to such **Gnosis of an Oasis**!! Did they Lock out their existential awareness due to Agnosia's?

Gnosia of what is Locked In within each one of us may show us the True and Untapped Human Potentials.

What or who will show us the way to unlock what is locked within? It required an Einstein to show the Humans the power of an Atom, the Nuclear Potential.

Will any Master lead the Humans to uncover the '**The Lost Realms**' or what is called the *Power of the Unconscious portions in their Minds!*

I wondered why Humaniforms must have that Privilege of inner discovery. ***Am 'I' as the Virion, not given that opportunity by the Creator?*** Are my progenies deprived of the 'Growth genes'? Are they made impotent to not transform to Stardom?

Will my Progenies, the Versions and Variants only face Crises and Doom? The *Parental anxiety* was rising in me, perhaps.

May be Human species started off as Viruses. They were introduced to this earth by an asteroid from space or a broken fragment from another planet which collided with this Earth. '*Humivirus*' seemed a funny word to me. They spread through the animal kingdom like a pandemic. After some time Humivirus got bored of globalization of itself. They became endemic in certain areas, especially chimpanzees, may be some gorillas and some monkeys.

Humivirus worked hard on these host bodies. They mutated and integrated their genes into the Apes genome pool. This corruption of the Apes genome pool forced them to change for survival. For this to happen, Apes had to choose to Accept and live with the virus, not fight it out.

Humivirus and apes evolved together into a beautiful byproduct called Homo Sapiens, the Human species.

Wow. I could envision the same endless possibilities for myself, I thought.

Prion messaged "Your Fantasies are creating sparks in the Nerve junctions, jarring sensations. This is disturbing my work. If this continues, you may attract Microglia, the scavenger cells or cause seizures for patient doc."

I apologized to Prion, but secretly within me, I began nurturing the **Imago** of a Virion idealizing the potentials within my nucleus. My unconsciousness could be a source of a sleeping yet giant intelligence. And I could aspire for a Dominion status on this Earth. But how!!

Who will be my Master? Patient doc!

I was hibernating within his Brain now. His Brain space felt like a Womb to me. I was Quarantined here to grow. This locked in state now seemed to be like the moments of **Dawn for 'I'**. My fate onto a Dominion status or into oblivion, to perish. But I felt a strong sense of Intensity within me, which meant 'I' owed no subservience to the Human Kind.

Echo appeared "You are now able to expand your Intelligence, your Vibratory quality of thinking is sharp, your mind has expanded sensitization of emotions and refined feelings of expression. Part of this is the effect of Patient docs energies, the **aura** his brain centers generate. His **Pineal Gland** is the port in the shape of a receptacle, at which my energies intersect with his Intelligence."

Echo parted saying "Don't try to imitate or Ape the Journey of Humankind. They had their trajectory. You form your trajectory. Be humble, if possible."

My Progenies will learn and earn for what I do. The Karmic Baggage. This distinct voice came from my Nucleus, my Soul. My Inner Gnosia!

I stayed in Silence; then heard a Voice, distinct and delightful, different from Echo. I did not know if this was coming from within me or outside me, from the ecosystem of the Brain.

"*The Voice from your own Soul is called Conscience; the Awareness that comes from it is called Spiritual Gnosia*. I am glad you are safe and learning quickly in your path of Self-discovery. I invite you to visit my Pineal Gland, when Prion is ready to facilitate your transport from current location."

First the surprise, then the flash of thought in me, "*Was this message originating from Patient Doc's subconscious?*"

I needed to wait for Prion's return from his scientific research work. I needed his validation and further co-operation.

I the Virion had **Gender Agnosia**. My species did not have the Gene to divide the species into male and female variants. I and my Progenies are Asexual. We replicate and reproduce by duplication of our mind and bodies. I heard that Worms are asexual too and reproduce through fragmentation.

Thankfully, we had no *Gender Wars* and no scope for forming Hybrids. No Hybrids of the Mind or Body meant no more Excess Diversity of the subspecies. I felt closer to the Universal Consciousness, which is Gender Neutral. We do not seek Mating partners!

A spark flashed from Pineal gland, then turned into a voice module, "Are you sure of this concept?"

I did not react, but thought to myself 'At least, I believe so.'

I missed Prion, not for validation on this matter. I waited for Prion, as a discussion partner. A partner with whom I had Trust and Patience to Wait!

Echo announced "You are growing graciously so far. **Equity** of your Sense and Sensibilities from Thinking, Emoting and Feeling are well spaced and connected to form Alignments in the Mind."

Echo continued "Well aligned features of the Natural Self and the Acquired Persona is the expected milestone of Youth. From here, you must experience and evolve to manifest a functional Society, Policies, Principles, and a Disease-Free ecosystem."

Could I be sure of my response abilities, I felt Self-doubt? But I will surely attempt.

Echo made a comment before parting, "**Jumping Genes** are real. These are mobile DNA, also named TRANSPOSABLE ELEMENTS (TE's). Known as Selfish Gene Elements they are important in genome function and evolution."

TE's make the evolution of Life unpredictable, beyond the grasp and controls of Intellect and Minds. They introduce Dynamism into the Psycheof the species.

Are '*Jumping Genes*' the residues of ancient viruses in human system, I wondered...

****

Glossary

- **Amnesia** – deficits, loss, or block in the access of memories from conscious and alert functions.
- **Ancestral** – of the past, transmitted from predecessors to current successor.
- **Archetypal** – an original thing from which others are copied.
- **Awareness** – a state of active intelligence of individuals being sensing, perspective and perceptions.
- **Blood Brain Barrier** – a special system of cells that form a membrane covering the nerve tissues and regulates the transport and access to toxic substances in the Blood. Functions like a Border.
- **Broca's** – region of the brain associated with production of speech.
- **Catastrophic** – an event or thing that causes great harm, suffering or destruction.
- **Civilizational** – an advanced stage or state of social evolution.
- **Cogito** – thinking as a principle of awareness and existence.
- **Conditional** – a matter, action or event that is co-dependent on another thing.
- **Consciousness** – original, intrinsic and Primary Intelligence within each organism.
- **Controversion** – against a version or versions
- **Dawn** – beginning of growth in manifestation of something or event. A Period when first light appears in the Sky.
- **Delusions** – a false image, belief or perception strongly

held in spite of invalidating evidence.

- **Digi-Social** – a way of connecting and interacting in society through digital platforms.
- **Digital** – an electronic system that uses numbers to generate, store and process data.
- **Dissociation** – separation of some interconnected parts of a system, which leads to dysfunctions.
- **Dominion** – power and authority to preside and govern over.
- **Dynamism** – great energy, power, drive to make things happen or make things succeed.
- **Economy** – a system of interrelated production and consumption activities. Sharing and Trade are parts of economic model of Life.
- **Elements** – basic or important part of a whole thing.
- **Epilogue** – is an overview or extract of information, usually added at the end of play.
- **Equity** – value of the share invested by the Individual Person, Entity or Group.
- **Ergo** – meaning, therefore.
- **Extroversion** – an attitude to experiencing Life by relating it through social and cultural norms.
- **Existential** – relating to and dealing with human forms and experience of external reality.
- **Fidelity** – quality of faithfulness or loyalty to some aspect of Life.
- **Foresight** – awareness of something before an event or experience happens or occurs.
- **Free Will** – power or ability to make own decisions in Life and Existence, without being controlled by Meta human powers or external human or environmental forces.
- **Fugue** -disturbance or dissolution of a person's mental

identifications and existential image associated with a flight from his usual environmental associations and habituations.

- **Gnosis** – awareness based on one own direct experience and Imperience.
- **Hindsight** – awareness of something after an event or experience has happened and passed.
- **Illusions** – a misleading image, idea, or perception.
- **Intent** – action that has purpose, design and determination behind it.
- **Introversion** – an attitude to experiencing Life by relating it through own contents of Psyche.
- **Insight** – awareness of something during the event or experience as is happening and unfolding.
- **Legacy** – transfer or inheritance of something produced or gathered by people in the past to one in the present.
- **Legion** – gathered or collected major unit of an army.
- **Lobes** – parts of the brain that are anatomically distinct and seem separately identifiable.
- **Messiah** – unique individual who functions as Savior, Rescuer or Liberator of people.
- **Micro-expression** – fleeting, involuntary facial expressions or mannerisms that may reveal private thoughts or emotions.
- **Microglia** – type of cells located throughout brain and spinal cord.
- **Neuropolitical** – domain of awareness investigating the interplay between different lobes and functions of Brain.
- **Nomadic** – not fixed to one place or habitation.
- **Orthodox** – approach to existential Life based on established and validated norms and conventions.
- **Oxymoron** – combination of two words that carry

opposite meanings.

- **Paradox** – contrary, distinct approach to existential Life which is strange to validated norms and conventions.
- **Perception** – the ways of grasping, organizing, and interpreting the events and experiences of the World. It is existential and interactive in its process and content.
- **Personality** – sets of temperaments, behaviors and conduct which helps an individual manifest their Inner energies and Character.
- **Perspective** – a way or mode of thinking, emoting, and acting based on inner Sense and Sensibilities.
- **Pineal Gland** – a small cone shaped structure in the center of the brain. It produces melatonin hormone which regulates the biological (circadian rhythm) clock in our body.
- **Psychiatrist** – medical doctor using allopathic practices to diagnose, prevent or treat Mental and Brain disorders and dysfunctions.
- **Psychobabble** – form of language used by people who talk about emotional and mental problems without accuracy and relevance.
- **Psychosomatic** – a distress, disease or disorder that originates from Psyche and transmits through to the Soma. Soma means the entire biological body except the reproductive cells.
- **Sabbatical** – a period of time for a break or change from routine affairs or efforts.
- **Sacrosanct** – something too important or too special to be changed or violated.
- **Scapegoating** – practice of singling out a person or group for unmerited blame and consequent negative treatment.
- **Schema** – representation of a concept or plan in the

form of an outline, framework, or model.

- **Spam** – unwanted, irrelevant, misdirected messages or communication to the Brain or Mind.
- **Spiritual** – coming from or of the Spirit, which is the Life creating energies in nature.
- **Splitting** – to divide or break a thing, a group or a whole system into smaller portions.
- **Temperament** – disposition or tendencies in reacting to environment and external data.
- **Trait** – a specific characteristic of an Individual's Self or Persona; determined by Genes.
- **Transposable** – capable of changing its location in gene and hence the sequencing.
- **Trauma** – impact of an event or experience which causes injury to body, brain, mind, or intellect.
- **Virion** – the complete, mature, functional unit of virus outside host cell.
- **Wernickes** – region of the brain associated with comprehension of speech.

Printed by Libri Plureos GmbH in Hamburg, Germany

9 798889 865308